Hooray
for Grandma
Jo!

Hooray for Grandma Jo!

by Thomas McKean

illustrated by Chris L. Demarest

CROWN PUBLISHERS, INC., New York

For my grandmothers—

Edith Heimann Mayer
and
Catherine Sheehan McKean

T. McK.

For Shirley and Grandma J.
with love

C. L. D.

Published by Crown Publishers, Inc., a Random House company, 201 East 50th Street, New York, New York 10022

CROWN is a trademark of Crown Publishers, Inc.
Manufactured in Singapore

Library of Congress Cataloging-in-Publication Data
McKean, Thomas.
Hooray for Grandma Jo! / by Thomas McKean ; illustrated by Chris Demarest.
p. cm.
Summary: Having lost her glasses, Grandma Jo mistakes an escaped lion for her grandson and takes him home with her, an action that leads to surprising results. (1. Lions—Fiction. 2. Grandmothers—Fiction. 3. Humorous stories.)
I. Demarest, Chris L., ill. II. Title. PZ7.M19415Ho 1994
(E)—dc20   93-16376
ISBN 0-517-57842-5 (trade)
0-517-57843-3 (lib. bdg.)

10 9 8 7 6 5 4 3 2 1   FIRST EDITION

One day, Grandma Jo received a letter from her daughter Elinor.

It said:

Dear Grandma Jo,
I have to go away for a week. If it's all right, I'll send little Lloyd to stay with you. He'll arrive next Tuesday on the 10:30 train, and he'll be wearing his new coat with the fluffy collar.
Love,
Elinor

"Goody!" said Grandma Jo. "My grandson is coming to visit!"

But that night, while she was making stew for dinner, Grandma Jo lost her glasses. She liked to dance while she cooked, and her glasses went flying off. She couldn't find them anywhere.

The next day, Grandma Jo got another letter. But she couldn't read it without her glasses.

"No matter," she said. "When little Lloyd comes, he can read it for me."

Here's what the letter said:

Dear Grandma Jo,
I don't have to go away after all, so little Lloyd won't be coming next Tuesday.
Love,
Elinor

But Grandma Jo couldn't read the letter!

Soon it was Tuesday. In the morning the newspaper came. Here's what it said:

THE NEWEST NEWS

Angry Lion Escapes!

An angry lion escaped yesterday from the city zoo. He was last seen heading in the direction of the train station. He is a mean lion. Just last week he bit a girl eating an ice cream cone. The zookeepers think that he is out of control. If you see this angry lion, make sure you call the police right away!

But Grandma Jo couldn't read the newspaper!

At ten o'clock,
Grandma Jo left for the train
station. She knew the way by heart. That's why she
could get there without her glasses.

When she got to the train station, it seemed empty.

But then she saw someone in a fluffy collar sitting in the waiting room. "Why, there's little Lloyd!" said Grandma Jo. "And my, how he's grown!"

So she took him home.

When they got inside, Grandma Jo said, "Now, little Lloyd, don't you want to take off your coat with the fluffy collar?"

"Grrr," said the lion.

"All right, dear," said Grandma Jo. "You can keep it on if you want to. Why don't we go outside and play on the swings?"

But when the lion got on the swing, he was so heavy he broke the whole swing set!

"You certainly weigh a lot for a little boy," said Grandma Jo.

"Now," said Grandma Jo, "I think it's a good time for your bath. You got a bit dirty when you were playing."

But the lion wouldn't get in the tub.

"No wonder you smell funny," said Grandma Jo. "Let's just forget about that bath and have dinner instead."

For dinner, there was a big plate of carrots. The lion
threw the entire plate right out the window!

"Goodness, dear," said Grandma Jo. "I thought you
liked carrots! Maybe we should skip to dessert."

For dessert, Grandma Jo brought out six flavors of ice cream to choose from.

The lion gobbled down all six in two seconds flat.

After that, he put his head in Grandma Jo's lap and sighed happily. "My word," said Grandma Jo. "You certainly do like ice cream!"

After dinner, Grandma Jo said, "Why don't we play a little before it's time for bed?"

First they played hide-and-seek . . .

Then Grandma Jo put on a record, and she and the lion danced . . .

Then Grandma Jo played the piano, and the lion played the drums . . .

And then they jumped
up and down on the sofa.

"My goodness!" said
Grandma Jo. "Don't we have
lots of fun together!"
Then Grandma Jo and the
lion went upstairs.

"Goodness gracious!" said Grandma Jo. "I guess we left your suitcase at the train station." So Grandma Jo helped the lion on with a pair of Lloyd's pajamas she always kept just in case.

"Golly!" said Grandma Jo. "You seem to have outgrown these pajamas. Now good night, dear."

And Grandma Jo kissed the lion good night.

"Prrrrrrr," said the lion.

During the night, someone else came to visit . . . and it wasn't a friend. It was Sneaky Sam, the burglar!

After Sneaky Sam had stolen all of Grandma Jo's old and pretty things, he thought he'd stop in the kitchen and have a snack.

He decided to eat some ice cream.

The sound of someone slurping ice cream woke the lion.

He went bounding downstairs into the kitchen.

When Sneaky Sam saw the huge lion, he became so scared he began to scream—and this woke up Grandma Jo.

Grandma Jo was so scared to hear someone screaming that she called the police.

In a second the police arrived.

"Goodness!" said Sergeant Hill. "We've not only caught Sneaky Sam the burglar, but we've also caught the runaway lion!"

"Nonsense!" said Grandma Jo. "That's my grandson, Lloyd. We've been having fun together all evening."

Then Sergeant Hill noticed Grandma Jo's glasses
sticking out of the stewpot.

"Maybe if you used your glasses, you would see it's
really the runaway lion," said Sergeant Hill.

So Grandma Jo put on her glasses and took a long look.

"My word!" she said. "I thought he seemed big for a little boy."

"That's a dangerous lion," said Sergeant Hill. "He must be sent away because he bit a little girl eating an ice cream cone, and we don't allow mean animals in the zoo."

But Grandma Jo thought about all the fun things she and the lion had done. She said to Sergeant Hill, "He is not a dangerous lion, just a hungry one who loves to eat ice cream. I bet he bit the little girl by mistake. Feed him ice cream and you'll find he's a perfectly nice lion."

Grandma Jo was right. The lion became as nice as he could be as long as he got all the ice cream he wanted.

Grandma Jo also got a big reward for catching Sneaky Sam. She gave the money to the zoo so they could buy all the ice cream they needed.

The directors of the zoo were so happy that they gave a big party in honor of Grandma Jo and the lion. Everybody came—even little Lloyd.

And here's what was written in the newspaper:

Grandma Jo Tames Angry Lion!

Grandma Jo tamed the angry lion by feeding him ice cream.

"We never could have done it without Grandma Jo," said the zookeeper. "She showed us what a good lion he really is!"

Hooray for Grandma Jo!